THE ADVENTURES OF MISS ANNE DE BOURGH OF ROSINGS

A PRIDE & PREJUDICE VARIATION
PREQUEL TO MR. DARCY'S BOOKSHOP

v. II

SUMMER HANFORD

COPYRIGHT

This is a work of fiction. Names, characters, businesses, places, events, locales, and incidents are used in a fictitious manner and researched for historical accuracy in so far as this author was able. Fictitious names, characters, businesses, places, events, locales, and incidents are products of the original work *Pride & Prejudice* or of this author's imagination. Any resemblance to reality is coincidental.

Also by Summer Hanford
*Mr. Darcy's Bookshop**
*The Adventures of Miss Anne de Bourgh of Rosings v. I**
*Mr. Darcy's Matchmaker**
*Once Upon a Time at Pemberley**

By Renata McMann & Summer Hanford
To Catch a Poisoner
Charitable Endeavors
*Pride & Prejudice and Planets**
*To Fall for Mr. Darcy**
Mr. Collins' Will
More Than He Seems
After Anne
Their Secret Love
*A Duel in Meryton**
Love, Letters and Lies
*The Long Road to Longbourn**
*Hypothetically Married**
The Forgiving Season
The Widow Elizabeth
Foiled Elopement
Believing in Darcy
Her Final Wish
Miss Bingley's Christmas
Epiphany with Tea
Courting Elizabeth
The Fire at Netherfield Park
*From Ashes to Heiresses**
Entanglements of Honor
Lady Catherine Regrets
A Death at Rosings
Mary Younge
Poor Mr. Darcy
Mr. Collins' Deception
The Scandalous Stepmother
Caroline and the Footman

Elizabeth's Plight (The Wickham Coin Book II)
Georgiana's Folly (The Wickham Coin Book I)
The Second Mrs. Darcy

Joint Collections:

A Dollop of Pride and a Dash of Prejudice:
Includes from above: *Their Secret Love, Miss Bingley's Christmas, Epiphany with Tea* and *From Ashes to Heiresses.*

Pride and Prejudice Villains Revisited – Redeemed – Reimagined A Collection of Six Short Stories.
Includes: *Lady Catherine Regrets, Mary Younge, Mr. Collins' Deception* and *Caroline and the Footman,* along with two the additional flash fiction pieces, *Mrs. Bennet's Triumph* and *Wickham's Journal.*

Georgiana's Folly & Elizabeth's Plight: Wickham Coin Series, Volumes I & II
Includes from above: *Elizabeth's Plight* and *Georgiana's Folly.*

By Renata McMann
Why Wed

Heiress to Longbourn
Pemberley Weddings
The Inconsistency of Caroline Bingley
Three Daughters Married
Anne de Bourgh Manages
The above five works are collected in the book:
Five Pride and Prejudice Variations

*available as an audio book

THE ADVENTURES OF MISS ANNE DE BOURGH OF ROSINGS v. II

CHAPTER ONE

Late Summer, 1798, Matlock Estate in Derbyshire

Anne sat beside Mrs. Jenkinson in Sir Lewis's spacious carriage and tried not to swing her feet. Apparently, young ladies of fifteen did not swing their feet. At least, not according to Mrs. Jenkinson, who had advised Anne that she was the beginning, middle, and end of any argument pertaining to manners.

In her mind, Anne recited fencing poses, struggling to remain still, but energy reverberated through her. They'd been in her father's carriage for hours. Days, really. The journey from Kent to Matlock wasn't a short one, although Father seemed happy with their time.

Finally, they rolled to a halt outside Uncle Matlock's big, old, gargoyle adorned manor house. Anne reached for the carriage door, eager to be free.

Mrs. Jenkinson's voice halted her with, "Ladies wait for a footman to open the door and assist them down."

"Ladies must be exceedingly lazy," Anne countered and flung open the carriage door to the sight of a startled footman.

Recovering quickly, he extended a hand.

With a grumpy look for Mrs. Jenkinson and an amused-looking Sir Lewis, Anne permitted the footman to help her down. The moment her hessians touched the gravel drive, she encountered a new trial...the deep desire to run in absolutely any direction, simply to be moving.

Instead, she waited while Mrs. Jenkinson and her father disembarked, then walked decorously up the grand steps with them and into the equally ostentatious entrance hall.

"Uncle, Cousin, Mrs. Jenkinson," Cousin Henry greeted with a bow as servants came forward to assist with their outerwear, little that they had in the late summer heat. "Father asked me to apologize as he is concluding some business. He will greet you all in the jade drawing room prior to supper, in two hours' time. I am to tell you, as well, that your usual rooms have been made ready, and the sitting room attached to Anne's chambers set aside for your private use."

"Thank you, Henry. That suits us well." Sir Lewis gestured up the staircase, his gaze shifting to take in Anne and Mrs. Jenkinson. "Ladies, shall we?"

"If I may borrow Anne, Richard asked to see her. He is working as well, in the library."

Anne stepped forward eagerly. She had little use for her cousin Henry, but she looked forward to seeing Richard.

"Very well," Mrs. Jenkinson said. "But do not tarry over long, Miss de Bourgh. You will need to change for dinner." Her critical gaze swept over Anne's travel gown, then dropped down to take in her boots.

"I will only exchange a quick greeting with my cousins," Anne assured her companion, in no way meaning her words. In truth, Anne meant to do precisely as she pleased, be it ready for dinner or, hopefully, anything more entertaining.

Mrs. Jenkinson's look of resignation clearly expressing what she thought of Anne's reassurance, she nodded. She and Sir Lewis started up the stairs to their rooms.

Anne grabbed Henry's arm and tugged him down the corridor, out of earshot, before demanding, "Why didn't Richard come greet us?"

"That's what I need to speak with you about." Shaking free of her grip, Henry grabbed her arm in turn and yanked her into a dark little parlor.

Anne looked about, suspicious. Henry could be hiding any sort of prank in the near darkness. "Say what you have to say, then."

"It's Richard. He needs our help."

Anne frowned, even more suspicious. What better way to lead her into a trap, possibly to a spot beneath a bucket of ink or some such, than to say that Richard needed her? "I thought you said he's working in the library."

"He is. He has been for weeks. It's awful and we must help him."

Anne raised her gaze in silent supplication. "You are making even less sense than usual, Henry."

Henry paced away in the dark room, pushing both hands through his hair. "It started this summer. This *thing* with Richard and Missy Steepleton, the parson's daughter."

"Sissy Missy?" Anne was familiar with the scrawny blonde girl, perhaps a year older than her, who used to try to play with them but who was always too afraid to do anything fun. Missy wouldn't hold frogs. Missy wouldn't climb trees. Missy squealed if mud touched her hem. "Richard has a...*a thing* with Missy?" The idea was absurd. Missy Steepleton was worthless as a companion.

But Henry paused his pacing, nodding with grave seriousness. "He fancies he's in love with her."

Anne wrinkled her nose. "Ugh. How horrible."

Henry eyed her curiously. "Love in general or with Missy Steepleton in specific?"

"Both." Anne could think of few things worse than being afflicted with love, but being afflicted with love for someone who grew queasy at the sight of a fish being gutted or a pheasant being plucked was one of them. "How did this happen?"

Henry shrugged. "The usual way. Lately Missy, you know…" He trailed off, making an hourglass sort of gesture. "She—"

"So help me, if you say 'blossomed,' I will punch you in the face."

Henry smirked. "You're just afraid because it's bound to happen to you."

At fifteen, Anne was acutely aware that it was happening to her, but no amount of *blossoming* would keep her from riding, fishing, hunting, and fencing. She imagined becoming a young lady hadn't changed Missy much, either. She probably still fainted at the sight of blood, even rabbit blood, and enjoyed needlepoint, or some such. Anne had never troubled to find out Missy's passions.

Because it was none of her business what Missy enjoyed, or of Henry's. "As useless as Missy is, it's not truly our concern. It is not as if we can dictate who Richard fancies."

"I don't care who Richard fancies," Henry said in an offensively exasperated voice, for it was not Anne's fault that her cousin could not properly convey information. "I care about the bargain Richard struck with Father."

"What bargain?"

"Remember how, last year, you and Richard and

Darcy dumped ink on me?"

Anne grinned. "I do."

Henry cast her a sour look. "Well, remember how Father said he would buy Richard a commission because he's obviously not suited for the priesthood?"

Anne's smugness grew, for she'd been quite pleased with that. Richard had always wanted to serve in the regulars, but hadn't, until then, been able to convince his father to agree with the notion. Healthy as Henry was, Richard was the spare, and the earl seemed inclined to keep him safe in case he was needed. "I remember that, too."

"Well, Richard has it in his head that he's in love with Missy and wants to marry her."

Anne gasped. It was one thing to be enamored with a girl, but another altogether to leap into a union with her. "What? He's too young to marry. Surely Uncle Matlock said no."

"He did, and not only because Richard is only seventeen. He said a son of his can do better than a parson's daughter, too."

Relief washed through Anne at her uncle's snobbery being put to good use. "So there's no trouble. Richard will enter into service soon, and while he's off fighting for the King, he'll forget all about Missy."

But Henry was shaking his head. "Ever since that night you inked me, Father has regretted his words. He's tried to talk Richard back into the priesthood."

"But Richard has always wanted to serve."

"Will you let me talk?" Henry demanded.

Anne pulled a face at him, but nodded.

"So," Henry paused, glaring at her to test if she would interrupt. After a moment, he continued, "So

Richard made a deal with our father. He says he will become a priest if Father will let him marry Missy."

"Uncle Matlock agreed to that?" The words burst out of Anne, full of incredulousness, and she clamped her hands over her mouth. She cast a quick look over her shoulder at the open parlor doorway, hoping no one was near enough to hear her. In a lower voice, she hissed, "How could he?"

"I guess he would rather have a live son who married beneath him than a dead one," Henry said quietly. With a sigh of resignation, he dropped down onto a settee that appeared too delicate for his thick limbs.

"Richard will not die if he serves," Anne said firmly. "He will be an excellent officer. The sort our nation needs. He will do great things and come home a hero, and be able to do much better, indeed, than Missy Steepleton."

"All I know is that he's constantly in the library studying and he says he's off to Cambridge this autumn."

"It is only Cambridge," Anne mused, dropping into a chair. "He can forget about her there, too, and still have plenty of time to take a commission."

Henry shook his head. "Father is having a contract drawn up. His side says that he will agree to an engagement when Richard leaves for Cambridge, and that they may be married as soon as Richard has the signatures of three respected theologians approving him to be ordained. Richard's part says that in exchange, he will never take a commission. Father is with his solicitors now, working on the details."

"Now?" Anne surged to her feet. Why hadn't Henry mentioned the matter was urgent? "I must speak with

Richard."

Anne rushed from the room, knowing the way to the library quite well. She could hear Henry's heavier tread following but didn't slow so he could catch up. A part of her still worried this was some sort of trick. After all, Richard had longed to serve since they were small. He wouldn't give up his life's dream for a bit of muslin-clad fluff.

Would he?

Anne burst into the library to the sight of Richard at a long table, surrounded by books. He stared at her, a pen in hand, poised over notes he'd obviously been writing. With a huff he blew out air to dislodge a swath of too-long brown locks from his eyes. His gaze went to the mantel clock.

Returning his attention to her, he smiled. "Anne. My apologies. I did not realize you had arrived. It is good to see you."

Noting that he did not put up his pen, she barreled up to the table. "Richard. Whatever are you doing?"

He looked down at the books, open and closed, and the messy pages before him, most scribbled on illegibly. "I'm studying. I'm going to be ordained. Like father wants." A drop of ink fell from the pen tip to splash down on the page before him. "Drat."

"Why under the sun would you want to be ordained?" Anne demanded.

Richard raised his gaze from the blot of ink. "So I can be married. Congratulations are in order. I will be engaged soon." He grinned foolishly.

This was worse than she'd thought. She'd never seen Richard appear so addlebrained. Not even when they'd stolen a bottle of brandy so they could learn to drink properly, like their fathers did. "I suppose congratulations are in order, then. Who is the wonderful miss soon to be your betrothed?"

"Miss Melissa Steepleton." Richard let out a long sigh, appearing even more lacking in sense than before.

"Missy Steepleton? The girl who cast up her breakfast on your new boots when you tried to show her a trout you'd caught?" Which hadn't been as large as the trout Anne caught at all, as she recalled.

"The very one. I love her."

"I see." She could tell by his horrendously besotted expression that there would be no reasoning with him, but still she ventured, "But what about taking a commission in the regulars? What about serving King and Country and visiting far away lands, and fighting the French?"

Richard plunked the pen down on the blotter, his expression suddenly glum. "Well, I truly did want to do that. You know being an officer embodies everything I care about. Well, that is, everything I used to care about. Now I care about Missy."

"Yes. Well, I am certain that is important, too."

Dejectedly, Richard added, "And she likes a man in regimentals. She told me she'd much rather marry a soldier than a priest, especially as her papa is one."

"So go be a soldier," Anne urged.

Richard shook his head, his face taking on a firm, set look. "No. If I do that, my father won't give me permission to marry. Missy and I would have to wait until I'm one and twenty, or maybe even until she is. That's another five years."

"What are five years if you are in love?"

Richard cast her an incredulous look. "I cannot imagine you waiting for anything for five years, de

Bourgh."

"Yes, but you are far more reasonable than I am."

Richard capped the inkwell, then reached for a cloth to clean the pen. "Not in this. Missy and I are in love and we want to be married, and that is the end of it."

"But your dream of—"

"I said that is the end of it," Richard reiterated firmly.

That most certainly was not the end of it, but Anne could see she would do no more good arguing with Richard about it now. "Very well, then. I am happy you have found love."

"Thank you," Richard said gravely.

Henry took that moment to finally enter, though he must have reached the library on Anne's heels. "There you two are," he said blithely. "It is time to ready for supper."

"You aren't my keeper," Richard replied, but he set down the cleaned pen and stood.

Anne followed her cousins from the library and up the front staircase. Something definitely had to be done. She would not permit Richard to throw away his dreams. Not on Missy Steepleton or any other girl. And to stop him, she would come up with the perfect plan.

CHAPTER TWO

Anne spoke very little at dinner, too preoccupied with her worry for Richard's future to attend to the conversation. Nor did he talk unless addressed directly, instead staring at nothing with a revoltingly moonfaced countenance. If it wouldn't have seen her sent from the table, Anne would have thrown roast carrots at him until he returned to reality.

Not that her father, uncle, or Henry seemed to note her and Richard's unusual silence, or Mrs. Jenkinson's typical quiet. All three men were enamored of their own voices and perfectly happy to dominate the conversation. Normally Anne would have taken exception and insisted on being heard, but she had more important matters on her mind than putting her relations in their place.

When dinner concluded she thought they would all adjourn to the drawing room, for they all knew better than to insist that as a female Anne must be banished from their presence, but Uncle Matlock rose and announced, "If you will excuse my poor manners, I must engage in a private word with Sir Lewis. We are off to my study to look over some papers I had drawn up today."

"Certainly, Father," Richard said eagerly.

Henry cast Anne a meaningful look.

"What papers, Uncle?" Anne asked.

Uncle Matlock sighed and turned to her father. "Lewis, she grows more impertinent every day. If you are not careful, even Darcy will not have her."

Anne smirked. "You adore my impertinence, but keep your papers secret if you like. I already know what's in them and I, for one, do not approve."

That earned her stifling looks from both her father and Richard.

Uncle Matlock scrutinized her for a moment with raised brows, then leveled narrowed eyes on Henry, who suddenly seemed to find a drop of gravy he'd left on the table linens exceedingly fascinating. With a snort, Uncle Matlock said, "Come along, Lewis," and tromped from the room.

After a final parting look of reprimand for Anne, her father followed his brother-by-marriage out.

Smiling brightly, Anne said, "Now, what shall we all do?"

Richard pushed back his chair, standing. "I am off to the library."

"No billiards?"

He shook his head. "I have far too much to memorize." He pulled a face. "And it isn't easy. Theology is so boring." His expression morose, Richard departed.

Anne swiveled to face Henry. "Billiards?"

"Very well."

"I will retrieve my sewing basket and join you in the billiards room," Mrs. Jenkinson said, rising from her place at the table.

"You do know that you needn't chaperone me with Henry?" Anne protested. It would be more difficult to formulate a plan to free Richard from his willful act of idiocy with Mrs. Jenkinson present.

"I wish to see if all your recent practice has paid off," Mrs. Jenkinson said before turning to the door.

Henry chuckled. "Been practicing, have you, de

Bourgh? Won't help, you know."

Anne left off glaring at Mrs. Jenkinson's departing form to say, "Or so you hope."

"Or so I know," Henry replied smugly.

"We will see." Her nose in the air, her hauteur only half-joking, Anne led the way from the dining room and down the hall.

Once they turned a corner, a pair of footmen trailing them a discreet distance, Anne slowed her pace. From the corner of her mouth, she muttered, "This thing with Richard is getting out of hand."

Henry pushed thick fingers through his curls. "Don't I know it. We need a plan, de Bourgh. Richard and I don't always get on, but I won't have my brother marrying a title grubbing little tart."

"Title grubbing?" Anne repeated. "Surely, she cannot imagine Richard will ever be earl?"

Henry cast a quick look over his shoulder, but the footmen who followed to see to their needs still maintained a polite distance. "No, but she wanted a title right enough. She tried her wiles on me not three weeks ago, but I'm not the fool Richard is."

Anne frowned. "Truly tried, or tried like how Miss Garter *tried* this past winter?" Obsessed with his role as heir, Henry thought any woman who so much as looked at him wanted to be his bride.

Henry cast her an annoyed glance. "What was I meant to think when she cast her fan at my feet?"

"That I'd knocked it from her hand after she called me clumsy." Anne was never clumsy. She simply hadn't learned one of the dances in the set yet. Since joining their household a little over a year ago, Mrs. Jenkinson had worked hard to transform Anne into a proper lady, but there was so much to learn and, as

Richard had said about theology, it was all terribly boring.

"Yes, well, I suppose I should have known that with you about, a lady's fan colliding with my shoe wasn't the lady's doing," Henry said sourly.

"Yes, you should have. You certainly didn't have to drag her over to the kissing bough." Anne chuckled. "Her betrothed was not amused."

"How was I to know she was spoken for?"

"Everyone else seemed to."

"I almost had to meet the fellow at dawn, all because you're clumsy."

Anne ground her teeth together. "Call me clumsy again and you will have to meet *me* at dawn." Sighting the billiards room door ahead, she drew in a calming breath. Quarreling with Henry wouldn't save Richard. "Tell me why you think Missy is title grubbing and I will decide."

They went in and Henry crossed to the far side of the room to rack the balls, the two footmen taking up position without. So they wouldn't have to speak loudly, Anne followed her cousin, coming to a halt beside the rack of cues.

"Well," Henry said quietly as he readied the table. "For a few weeks, she'd been popping up everywhere I went, so I was getting suspicious. Being heir to an earl, I've developed a knack for knowing when I'm being hunted, you know?"

Her back to Henry as she contemplated the cues, Anne raised her gaze heavenward in a silent bid for the strength to endure their collaboration.

"Then, one morning when I'm coming out of the stable, walking from the dark inside into the light, you know? She runs right into me. She was all apologetic but a few minutes later, I noticed a crinkle and there was a note in my coat pocket saying, 'Come to the old orchard. I'll be waiting.'"

Anne pulled down her favorite cue. "And you are certain she put the note there?"

"I wasn't, no, but I went, and there she was, and quite willing to be there, no mistaking." Henry grinned. "If you take my meaning."

Anne pulled a face. "No one has ever had trouble taking your meaning. Tell me you did not compromise the woman your brother might marry."

Henry waved that off. "Nah. Just a few kisses is all, and then she started whispering about marriage and I was away from there." He snorted. "Marry Missy Steepleton indeed. She's the parson's daughter. I'm heir to an earl. She was mad to even think it."

Fighting past her disgust with Henry, Anne said, "But this is perfect. You marry her, and Richard won't be able to."

"Just said I won't, didn't I?" Henry pulled down his usual cue. "You can break, being a girl and all."

"I will flip you for it," Anne said dryly, and dug her lucky cartwheel from her skirt pocket. Waggling it so Henry could see the profile of King George on one side and the trident-wielding goddess on the other, Anne said, "King or Britannia. You call," and tossed the coin.

"King George," Henry replied, predictably.

Anne snatched the coin from the air and slapped it down on the back of her hand, then lifted her other to reveal Britannia on her rock. She smirked at Henry and shoved the coin back in her pocket. "I guess I will break after all."

But Henry stepped into her way. "Look, what are we going to do about Richard?"

Anne lowered the butt of the cue to the floor, resting both hands atop it. "It's perfectly simple."

"I said I won't have her," Henry reiterated with a touch of volume and anger.

"I know." Anne paused, pulling her thoughts to her. "And you do not need to. We simply need to show Richard what sort of person she truly is. The sort who would move on to him after failing with you. That's not love. It's mercenary, and he will see that."

"I could show him the note."

"You still have it?" Anne asked, surprised.

Henry grinned. "I keep them all. Sort of trophies, aren't they?"

Anne wrinkled her nose, uncertain why anyone would think a union with Henry was worth a title. "Did she sign it?"

Henry shook his head. "We could get her to write something new, and sign it, and then show both notes to him. He will have to concede that the handwriting is the same."

"No. The first note isn't signed or, I imagine, even dated. She could pretend it's from years ago, or for a completely different purpose. He needs something irrefutable." She pressed her lips into a hard line, thinking. Would it be too reprehensible to lead Missy Steepleton on? But why not? She was playing games with Richard's life. "Do you believe you could get her to meet you in the orchard again? For some more kissing?"

"Definitely."

Grimacing at how certain Henry sounded, Anne said, "It seems overly cruel to do to her, but I'm afraid you will need to lure her there so Richard can catch her in the act."

"He'll hate me," Henry protested.

"He will thank you for showing him the truth about her before he makes a terrible error."

Henry scratched at the side of his head, his expression thoughtful. "That's true. He should thank me."

Anne contained another roll of her eyes. "And he undoubtedly will, once he's over the initial shock. We'll set up a meeting with Missy, and I'll make certain Richard discovers the two of you."

Turning a suddenly suspicious look on her, Henry said, "You'd best, and do not be late. I already told you, I'm not going to marry her. Not that Father would permit it."

"He's going to permit Richard to marry her," Anne protested.

"Richard is the spare," Henry said, shrugging as he stepped out of her way.

Putting all her annoyance with Henry into the shot, Anne broke, billiards balls smacking into one another with a satisfying clatter.

Mrs. Jenkinson appeared moments later, her sewing basket in hand, and Anne and Henry proceeded with the match, followed by several more. Henry won more than Anne did, but she didn't fare as poorly as usual against him, so she left the billiards room in a far more cheerful state than he did. Henry hated losing.

Running through various ideas for how to get Richard to the orchard when the time came, Anne went up to her room, walking side by side with Mrs. Jenkinson. When they reached her chambers, across the hall from her companion's, they both came to a halt.

"Do you require help with your hair?" Mrs. Jenkinson asked, by which Anne knew her companion meant, 'Can I count on you to brush and braid your hair so it does not become a bird's nest by morning?'

Having noted an abundance of light coming from under the door to the sitting room attached to her bedchamber, Anne shook her head. "Undoubtedly Sarah is waiting." Sarah, the maid Mrs. Jenkinson insisted Anne must have, had likely built up the fire in anticipation of her arrival and would see to her hair even if Anne attempted to avoid it. "Have a pleasant rest, Mrs. Jenkinson."

"I would rest easier if you had not been so quiet throughout dinner." Mrs. Jenkinson scrutinized Anne's face. "I become leery when you are silent."

Anne chuckled. "How silly you are."

"Yes. Hopefully," Mrs. Jenkinson replied and went into her room.

Grinning at Mrs. Jenkinson's worry, Anne opened the door to the sitting room…to the sight of her father seated in a chair by the fire. He had a book open in his lap, but held his monocle between a thumb and forefinger, a sure sign of agitation. When Sir Lewis was annoyed, he would tap his monocle against his book, or the arm of a chair, or whatever was handy. Often were the times the tap tap tap of the copper ring against wood had nearly driven Anne mad.

"Father, I did not expect to see you until morning," Anne said as she entered and closed the door behind her. "Is all well?"

He gestured her over. "Where have you been, young lady?"

"Playing billiards with Henry."

Her father sighed. "I would rather if you said

conspiring with Henry."

"And what would I be conspiring about?"

"Some way to prevent this nonsense with Richard."

Anne dropped to sit on the corner of the sofa that stood across from the fireplace. "So I was correct about what's in Uncle Matlock's papers?"

"Irrefutably."

"And you do not agree with his plans for Richard?"

Sir Lewis shook his head. "It is madness. I know he's worried for his son, but Richard as a parson? Utter nonsense. I have convinced Matlock to think on the matter for a few days more, but something must be done. I am afraid I may have to call in Darcy. This may require a conclave."

Anne had not thought of sending for Uncle Darcy. A solid plan, but only if he agreed with her father. Anne wasn't certain he would. Uncle Darcy always seemed keen on people getting married. "Well, if I *were* conspiring, you would be able to count on me to help Richard not make this mistake."

Sir Lewis nodded, appearing pleased. "That is all I wished to hear. I believe your maid is in your chamber waiting for you. Scared the poor thing off, I am afraid." He stood.

Anne did as well, and impulsively gave her father a hug. "Do not worry, Papa. We will put this matter right."

He patted her on the head. "I know we will. Rest well, Anne."

"And you." She followed her father to the door, then closed it softly behind him.

Crossing to her bedchamber, Anne smiled. She would put things right. They had a nice, simple plan. So simple, nothing could go wrong.

CHAPTER THREE

The following morning, Anne entered the library to the sight of Richard bent over his books, much like the day before. Making no effort to quiet the rap of her hessians on the polished floorboards, she crossed to stand before him.

"I'm working," he muttered, not looking up as he scrawled words on a piece of loose parchment, his free hand marking his place in some dusty old tome.

"I have excellent vision and keen observational skills," Anne replied. "There is absolutely no reason to state the obvious."

Hand stilling, he looked up with a frown, then blew out air to swish his too-long hair away from his eyes. "I meant my words more to reprimand than inform. Whyever you're here, the answer is that I'm far too busy. No matter how you feel about Miss Steepleton, I love her, and I have work to do." He returned his attention to the page before him.

Anne raised her gaze heavenward in silent supplication. "I am here to offer an olive branch."

Richard's head snapped back up, his eyes narrow. "You don't offer olive branches."

"Well I am, so consider yourself fortunate," Anne snapped, aware that anger would convince Richard of her sincerity far more quickly than any softer emotion.

"I don't feel lucky. I feel as if you're interrupting my work."

That did not deserve an answer. "Mrs. Jenkinson

and I are to call on Missy Steepleton this afternoon and I thought—"

"What?" Richard's eyes widened in alarm. "You are not to do anything to her, de Bourgh. No ink in her slippers or manure in her pillow or dye in her face paints or—"

"Don't be absurd," Anne cut in, offended.

"It is not absurd. You've done all those things to people. I know because I helped."

Anne scrunched her nose. "Precisely. I would never play the same prank twice. How mortifying. You know me better than that."

Richard assessed her for a moment, his serious mien making him look older than his seventeen years. "Then what are you planning? Why are you going to call on her?"

Yes, Richard looked older, Anne concluded, but certainly not old enough to marry. "Mrs. Jenkinson suggested I should come to know the woman Missy has grown into to better understand what you could possibly see in her." Or rather, Anne was certain Mrs. Jenkinson would make such a sensible suggestion if they'd conversed on the topic, which they had not. Mrs. Jenkinson couldn't be allowed to know Anne had any opinion on Missy at all, or she would surely ruin everything.

"Well," Richard said slowly, sitting back in his chair. "That makes sense. Mrs. Jenkinson is a good influence on you."

"Mrs. Jenkinson is tedious," Anne countered, though in truth she had a grudging respect for her companion. And, though Anne would die before admitting as much, she appreciated Mrs. Jenkinson's efforts to teach her decorum. She'd helped Anne to understand how much better she could sneak about when people saw what they expected to see in the daughter of Sir Lewis de Bourgh. "But if I must go to have tea with Missy, I thought you might like me to sneak her a note. The afternoon won't be a complete waste then."

"By which you mean that as you will be breaking at least some rules, you'll endure tea with another miss?" Some of his usual amusement had crept into Richard's voice, much to Anne's relief.

"Precisely," she agreed. "So, write something down and seal it up, or what have you. Tie it with a ribbon for all I care. I'll find a way to get it to her for you."

Richard's expression brightened with a disgusting amount of eagerness. "Truly? Because I'm forbidden to see her or even to write to her until I sign Father's contract, and your father is arguing with him over the details, holding things up."

"Truly." So as not to sound too eager, Anne added, "Even though this *thing* you have with Missy is nauseating."

Richard grinned and pulled free a clean sheet of paper. He penned the salutation, then looked up at Anne with raised eyebrows. "If I could have some privacy?"

Anne huffed and moved away, making a show of trailing her fingertip along the spines of a row of books to which she gave little attention.

As soon as Richard was engrossed in his letter, she inched around the room until she was behind him. Pivoting on now quiet feet, she sneaked up until she could read the letter. Her face crinkled at the drivel there. Embarrassed on Richard's behalf, she snorted.

His head came up. "I thought I made it clear that

you weren't to read this."

"And I wish I hadn't, but I cannot help but notice that you left out the most important bit."

He swiveled to face her. "Most important bit?"

"When and where she should meet you."

Richard's brows drew down in a dire vee. "I already told you, I'm forbidden seeing her."

"So? If you get caught, it's hardly as if your father can further forbid you. What could he do, force you to marry her sooner?"

"True, but it seems wrong to go against a direct order. Especially one to which I agreed."

Anne shrugged. "I suppose that's up to you. I'm certain Missy won't mind that you're a tepid lover."

"A tepid lover?" Richard exclaimed. His sweeping gesture took in the piles of notes and books. "I'm working every waking hour to secure our future as speedily as possible."

"But she doesn't see any of that, does she? All she knows is that your father ordered you to keep away for a time, and you are, and you aren't making any effort to see her." Anne sniffed. "Tepid."

With a scowl, Richard turned back to his letter. His strokes firm, he jotted, *I must see you. Two mornings hence, meet me in the old orchard on the border of your estate at eight, as we were wont to before I told my father of our love. My heart longs to hear your sweet voice. My eyes to gaze upon your—*

Pulling a face, Anne stopped reading. She didn't need to know what parts of Missy's anatomy Richard longed for. All she'd needed to do was to get him to pick a time and place to meet. If she had failed, it would have come down to convincing Missy instead, but of course she had not failed. She rarely did.

"There," Richard stated, signing his name with a flourish. "Tepid indeed."

Anne leaned over the page, pretending she hadn't already read his words. "Eight? So early?"

Richard yanked the letter away. "If you must know, she prefers to walk early, just as I do." Smugly he added, "It is only one of the ways in which we are perfect together."

Anne couldn't contain another snort but she did manage not to ask when Missy had discovered her love of walking early...before or after Richard had conveyed his feelings on the matter. "Why the orchard?" Was that not where she'd met with Henry?

"She's cultivated the notion that she enjoys preserves made from the old trees best, and goes to assess the progress of the apples often," Richard said absently, waving the page to help the ink dry. "It was her ready excuse, so we could meet."

Apparently, Missy Steepleton was more clever than Anne had realized, and very dedicated to securing a husband. Not that her dedication would matter when it came to Richard. Anne would foil her.

Richard folded the page into a square small enough to fit into Anne's palm, or into the pocket of a gown, sealed it, and held it out. His gaze serious, he said, "Thank you. I appreciate you taking Mrs. Jenkinson's advice regarding Miss Steepleton, and bringing her this. You're a good friend."

Anne smiled and took the letter. "You are welcome, Richard." She was a good friend. So much so that Missy Steepleton would never see Richard's letter, nor marry him, nor ruin his dream of being an officer.

Leaving the library, Anne asked around until she located Henry about to set out for his duck blind, his favorite spaniels and a servant in tow. Turning to the latter she said, "Samuel, please retrieve my fowling piece. Mrs. Jenkinson will know where it may be found. I am joining my cousin on his hunt."

"Must you?" Henry groused as the servant hurried away.

"I believe so. I both enjoy shooting and have need of a private word."

Henry's eyes brightened with interest and he nodded, making no more protest as Anne hurried away to secure her hat. Fortuitously, the gown she wore would do well enough and she already had her boots on. Also fortuitous was Mrs. Jenkinson's lack of desire to trek out into the marshes.

Side by side, Anne and Henry set out for the large pond that rested in a flat area to the west, dug ages ago to collect enough water to keep the surrounding fields and a small, now empty cottage, dry. A favorite of ducks, geese, and various other waterfowl, the murky basin often provided fresh meat for the earl's table, be it fowl or fish.

As they tramped through the tall grass, Henry asked, "So, you've found a way for me to show Richard what sort of scheming title hunter he's fallen for?"

"Hush," Anne hissed, looking about.

"Don't fuss at me, de Bourgh. Samuel is too far behind to hear and even the dogs aren't paying us any attention."

True though that was, Anne still spoke in a low voice as she replied, "Yes. You must meet Miss Steepleton in that old apple orchard at quarter till eight in the morning two days hence."

"Quarter till eight?" Henry exclaimed, making no attempt to modulate his voice. "You must be mad. I won't be out of bed yet."

Anne offered an impatient shrug. "Richard believes they will meet at eight, so you must be there before, so he can catch the two of you together."

"Quarter till eight," Henry muttered darkly. "The things I'm willing to endure for my baby brother."

"Or should we make your meeting earlier?" Anne asked. "Will a quarter of an hour be long enough for you to ensure that the two of you are in a compromising position?" She cast Henry a stern look. "Only remember, it must be clear that she is the one kissing you, not the other way around. Can you manage that in fifteen minutes?"

Henry chuckled. "I can manage it in five. But don't let Richard be late. I don't want things to go too far. As I said, I am not about to marry the girl."

"No one is going to marry Missy Steepleton," Anne declared, pushing aside an excessively tall clump of grass. "Just make certain you're in the orchard when you're meant to be." She would take care of the rest.

CHAPTER FOUR

Later that afternoon, after bagging two more ducks than Henry did, though he claimed she'd stolen one of his, Anne endured slippers and a day gown in order to call on the Steepletons. Mr. Steepleton was busy composing Sunday's sermon when Anne and Mrs. Jenkinson arrived, but his wife and daughter were more than happy to receive them. Anne felt a stab of relief, for she hadn't considered that Missy might not be at home.

The parson's dwelling in Matlock was larger than most such homes, and the drawing room into which Anne and Mrs. Jenkinson were shown was rather more opulent than might be expected. Anne supposed such grand surroundings were what gave Missy the notion that she could finagle the son of a peer into marrying her.

They entered to polite greetings and sat to the offer of tea, all while Anne studied Missy. If by 'blossomed' Henry meant that the poor girl had become burdened by a rather large bosom, she supposed her cousin was correct in his assessment of the change in Missy since last Anne was in her company. In all other ways, Missy still appeared to be the round faced, lightly freckled girl Anne recalled. So much so that she contained a grimace at the thought of Missy kissing Henry. Only three years her senior, he somehow seemed far older.

But Anne hardened her heart and plastered on a smile. Looking around the well-appointed room, done in puce and cream tones, she sought a way to speak with Missy alone before tea could arrive. Some ancient-looking embroidery hung on one wall offered little, but taking in a row of small, framed watercolors depicting the outside of the parsonage, Anne exclaimed, "Why, those are quite lovely. May I view them closer?"

Mrs. Jenkinson turned to her and Anne could sense her companion's suspicion even though her demeanor showed no change. "Those watercolors, Miss de Bourgh?" Mrs. Jenkinson knew she had no use for such clutter.

"Oh, my Melissa did those, did you not, dear?" Mrs. Steepleton turned to her daughter. "Missy, dear, show Miss de Bourgh your paintings."

Missy's face pinked and she looked down even as she rose. With a gesture at the paintings, she said, "If you would care to see them, Miss de Bourgh?"

"I would be delighted." Anne refused to even glance at Mrs. Jenkinson as she too stood.

"We're so pleased you've called," Mrs. Steepleton said as Anne and Missy turned away from the low table on which tea would be served. "Ever since young Mr. Fitzwilliam announced his intentions, well, we've worried that the earl is not entirely pleased."

"I am certain he simply wants what is best for his son, and for your daughter," Mrs. Jenkinson replied.

Somehow, Anne could feel her companion's gaze on her back as she and Missy crossed the room.

"Oh, yes, certainly." Mrs. Steepleton added a titter to her words, though Anne had no idea what about them might be meant to amuse.

"It is lovely weather we are enjoying, especially for the end of summer, do you not think?" Mrs. Jenkinson asked, directing the conversation to safer ground.

Mrs. Steepleton's reply was equally benign and the two fell into practiced, meaningless chatter as Anne and Missy crossed the room.

"They are all renditions of our home," Missy said when they reached the paintings.

Anne bent near the first one, pretending close examination. It bothered her that the watercolor was actually quite good. "Are they all from the same year?"

"Oh no. They are all in clement weather, because I did them out of doors, but you can see that this is several years ago. They become newer as we move to the right. Really, these older ones are rather embarrassing. I had no skill then."

Anne cast her an incredulous look but Missy seemed to be studying her clasped hands and gave no appearance of boasting. "You underestimate your talent."

Missy's gaze darted up. "Truly?"

Anne shrugged. "I do not tend to flatter."

A fleeting smile touched Missy's mouth. "I know. That is the first nice thing you have ever said to me. Usually it is, 'You blubber like a baby,' or, 'It's dirt, not rat poison.'" Missy dropped her gaze but, before Anne could respond, looked back up again to ask softly, "Are you being kind because Mr. Fitzwilliam wishes to marry me?"

"I complimented your talent because you have it," Anne replied, because even if she didn't like the other young woman, it bothered her that Missy couldn't see how skilled she was. "And I called today because my cousin urgently requires a word with you and knew no other means but to send me."

Missy's eyes brightened. "Richard?"

Anne moved to the next painting. It appeared to be

in summer, while the budding leaves in the first clearly marked it as spring, and was, indeed, executed with more skill. "No," she said in the barest whisper. "Henry. He says he must speak with you." Raising her voice she added, "You rendered the roses so expertly," and moved to an autumnal rendition.

"Henry?" Missy whispered.

Out of the corner of her eye, Anne took in Missy's frown. That would not do. "He told me that turning you away was his greatest mistake. That..." Anne repressed a grimace, but boldly pressed on with, "That he longs to make you a lady."

"Oh," Missy exclaimed, a hand going to her mouth.

"Is all well, dear?" Mrs. Steepleton called across the room.

Anne turned to smile at the two older women. "I pointed out where she's done the curtains wrong, though it is a very nice detail that she included them behind the windows."

"Oh, but they are not wrong," Mrs. Steepleton replied. "These are new." She smiled indulgently at her daughter. "Melissa would never make such an error."

"She is very skilled," Anne agreed. To Missy she said, "Is that the newest?" She drew them down the line of paintings, waiting for Mrs. Jenkinson and Mrs. Steepleton to return to their discourse on the weather.

"When?" Missy whispered.

"In two days, at quarter till eight in the morning, in the old orchard," Anne murmured back before more loudly asking, "Is that your cat sleeping in the window? So few strokes but you captured her presence there so well."

A clatter sounded at the other side of the room and Mrs. Steepleton announced, "Tea is here. Melissa, come serve. I am certain Miss de Bourgh and Mrs. Jenkinson will be impressed with your skill."

"Yes, Mama," Missy replied, turning back to the seating area, but before she stepped away she caught Anne's gaze and nodded.

Anne suppressed a grin, following Missy back. Everything was working out to perfection.

CHAPTER FIVE

Two days later, Anne rose with the sun. She rang for her maid to ask for tea and dry toast, and for someone to be sent to task Henry's valet with waking him. Her tray arrived just as she was finishing her morning ablutions, and she asked the girl who brought it to have Henry's valet check on his progress. She then proceeded to dine, sending another servant when she finished her toast.

Clad in a rather severe brown gown that she generally reserved for hunting, Anne then donned her boots. She was tying the second when a knock sounded on the door to the sitting room attached to her bedchamber. Her maid went to answer and Henry's voice reached Anne's ears. She yanked out her watch, frowned to see the time read quarter past seven, and went to ask him why he was knocking on her door when he should be off to the orchard.

Sighting her over the maid's shoulder, his expression grumpy and his eyes bloodshot, Henry said, "There you are, de Bourgh. Look, stop sending my valet to pester me. I'm up. I'm leaving."

"If you are up and leaving, you will not have to worry about your valet pestering you," she observed as she crossed the room. With a gesture, she sent the maid away.

Rather than grow more annoyed, as Anne expected him to, Henry chuckled. "True enough. But look, it's Richard who should be worrying you."

She frowned. "Richard? Has he changed his mind

about the meeting?" Had he gone all noble on Anne, refusing to go against his father's wishes?

Henry shook his head. "No. While you were setting my valet on me, I was sending him to spy on Richard. He's finishing his coffee as we speak, and means to depart with haste." Henry pulled a face. "Apparently, he's eager for Miss Steepleton's company. I don't need long alone with her but you must delay him for at least a few minutes."

Anne nodded. "I will, never fear."

"And it occurs to me that I could use some sort of signal to let me know when he's getting close. Just to make certain he sees what we mean him to. True form and all that."

"Right." She should have thought of that. "I will hoot like an owl."

"An owl? They won't be about this late in the morning."

Reining in her annoyance at having to explain, Anne replied, "Yes. Which is why when you hear one, you will know it's me and not a real owl."

Henry snorted. "Think a lot of your bird calls, do you?"

Anne took his shoulder and yanked, turning him around to face the hallway. "Go. I'll delay Richard and then follow him so I can sound the warning."

Henry nodded, adjusted his coat, and set off down the hall.

Anne closed the door, then hurried into the bedchamber to grab her hat. Taking it, she hastened back across the sitting room and peeked into the hall. Holding her breath, she slipped out, then softly closed the door behind her.

Mrs. Jenkinson would still be in her bedchamber.

Anne's earlier chatter with Henry wouldn't have troubled her, but Anne had learned that Mrs. Jenkinson had an inexplicable ability to know when she was sneaking. The last thing Anne needed was her companion interfering this morning.

Tiptoeing past Richard's door, Anne went to the top of the staircase. She lingered there, waiting. A few moments later, one of the doors in the hall opened. Anne looked back, ready to feign having forgotten something in her room if it was anyone other than Richard.

But it was him, striding down the hall in her direction. She pasted on a smile, waiting until he reached her to continue descending the staircase.

"A pleasant morning to you, cousin," she said as she fell in step beside him.

Richard's answering grin was somewhat foolish. "It is, and you know why. Thank you for orchestrating this."

Anne suppressed a wince of guilt. "Yes. About that." Jumping down the final two steps, she whirled to face him, halting him before his foot could touch the floor of the entrance hall. "Is it not a bit early? You don't want to seem too eager."

"But I am eager and there's no reason to prevaricate about it." He stepped around her.

Anne rushed after him as he started down the hall leading to the back of the house. "But you don't want to *seem* eager," she tried. "Women like the chase and all that. Mystery. A touch of danger."

"Being late rather than early would provide a touch of danger?" Richard's eyes were alight with amusement. "That's ridiculous."

Anne dodged ahead of him again, forcing him to

halt in a corridor rendered dark by snuffed out candles and a lack of natural light, the windows in the adjoining drawing room being west facing. "I am only trying to help, you know."

Richard's brows drew together. "Meaning no insult, de Bourgh, but you are the last person I would go to for advice on what women want."

Anne huffed, pretending anger. If she couldn't slow him with advice, maybe an argument would work. "I do happen to be one, and I am seriously offended by your remark."

"You are not." He made to step around her.

Anne matched the movement. "I am. I've been working diligently on being more ladylike. You have insulted me."

Richard's frown deepened as he studied her. Finally, he shook his head. "No, I have not."

"I ought to know if I'm insulted," Anne protested. How long has she bought Henry? With how slowly he usually walked, not enough time.

Richard's eyes narrowed dangerously. Then, breaking his glare, he looked up and down the hallway. Jabbing a finger in the direction of the open drawing room doors, he commanded, "In there. Now."

Anne wasn't impressed. The day Richard could intimidate her, she really would give up hunting, fishing, fencing, and everything she loved, and become a simpering socialite who only cared if her slippers matched the ostrich feathers sticking out of the top of her head. "No."

"Look, you are going to tell me what is going on here, or I am running to the orchard, and you know you can't catch me."

Anne ground her teeth. He was right. In a footrace,

Richard always won. No matter how she trained, he was taller, with longer legs. She couldn't keep up. "Very well. After you." She wouldn't be tricked into getting out of his way so he could run for it.

Shrugging, Richard pivoted and strode into the drawing room. He turned to face her as she followed. "Well? What are you planning to do to Missy? Have you set snares in the orchard? Or hid a basket of snakes in an apple tree?"

Anne couldn't help but chuckle at that. "Snakes in an apple tree? How biblical."

"I am serious, Anne. Either tell me what you have planned for my intended or I will be in that orchard faster than you can spell my name, and I'll unleash whatever you have waiting before Missy can."

Anne took in Richard's earnest, indignant face. She sighed. "I do not have anything planned for her. At least, not in the way you suspect. I simply want to reveal her true nature to you."

"What do you mean?" Richard asked, unease putting a quake in his voice.

"Henry has gone to meet her. He's going to let her kiss him." Anne took in the shock on Richard's face and braced for his anger.

His surprise melted into relief. "That's all? "Nothing is going to scare her or launch at her or spill on her?"

Stunned by his lack of ire, Anne merely shook her head.

"Then all will be well, and I am off to the orchard." He started past her, from the room.

"But...did you not hear me?" Anne asked, catching up to him. "She will be there kissing Henry."

"She will not. She has no interest in him."

"She does so." Anne hated to be the one to tell Richard but... "She tried her wiles on him before turning them on you. She does not care for you. She cares for your station. She wants to be a lady."

Richard merely shook his head as they continued on their way to the back of the house. "She told me of her brief infatuation with Henry. She did not know what love was then. Now she does. With me."

Where she walked beside Richard, working to keep her strides as long as his, Anne cast him an incredulous look. "You cannot believe that."

"Why wouldn't I?"

She didn't have a good answer to that. Her mind whirling, Anne sought a new facet of her plan. "So you are certain of Missy's love for you?"

"I am."

"She would never kiss Henry?"

Richard cast her an annoyed look as they reached a narrow door the staff often used to come and go from the back garden. "She would never kiss any man but me." He yanked the door open.

"You are confident in that?" Anne pressed, following him out.

"Very."

"Well, then, there is no harm in us sneaking into the orchard and taking a peek at the two of them."

Richard's steps slowed. He cast her a thoughtful look. "I do not want to spy on the woman I love."

"It sounds to me as if you aren't as confident as you want to be, then." Anne permitted a touch of taunting into her tone.

Richard flashed her an annoyed look. "Not so. It seems wrong, though, somehow. As if I don't trust her, and I do."

"Well, I do not. You must consider it a favor to me, and I will take all blame should Missy discover us." Anne yanked at her skirt. The aggravating thing made it difficult to keep up with her taller cousin.

"What if we have a deal, you and I?" Richard asked.

Anne left off fretting with her skirt. "What sort of deal?"

Richard did not reply and they walked in silence, the garden almost cold in the early morning air, hinting that autumn was not far off. Finally, as they moved from the carefully manicured grounds near the house onto a narrow trail, he said, "When we reach them and see that Missy has no interest in Henry, you will agree not to interfere between us again. Ever."

"And if I am right?"

"You will not be."

He seemed so certain, hope that he was correct intruded into Anne's surety. She pressed it aside. "But if I am right, then you will agree not to marry her."

"Very well."

Satisfied, Anne let the matter drop.

They did not speak again until they drew near the orchard, at which point Anne put a hand on Richard's arm, halting him.

He turned a questioning look on her.

"If we really mean to learn the truth, I suggest we move with more care," Anne said quietly.

Richard frowned his annoyance at her, but nodded.

Releasing his arm, Anne led the way into the orchard, slipping from tree to tree with careful stealth. Soon enough, they drew in sight of Henry and Missy Steepleton, who stood speaking beneath a tree. Cupping her hands about her mouth, Anne issued a sure, loud, "Hoot Hoot."

Henry's shoulders tensed, but he gave no other indication he heard. Missy appeared not to notice the sound. Richard cast Anne a suspicious look.

She glared back, gesturing that they should move closer.

CHAPTER SIX

Anne slipped through the cracked and weathered fruit trees, Richard at her side. She fought not to hold her breath, knowing that would render her shakier and less able to move in silence. As they inched forward, ducking gnarled branches and stalking from trunk to trunk, Missy's and Henry's voices coalesced into discernable words.

". . . happy you have changed your mind, my dearest Henry," Missy was saying as Anne touched Richard's arm to get his attention.

He looked over and she nodded to a pair of wide trunks. Richard nodded back and the two of them slipped behind the ancient apples to listen.

"It was seeing you with my brother," Henry rumbled, his voice pitched deeper than how he usually spoke.

Anne scrunched her nose. Was this Henry being . . . alluring? Gross.

Missy dipped her head so she could look up at Henry through her lashes. "Then I am so happy that you saw me with him."

Beside Anne, Richard vibrated with tension. A quick glance showed his usually amiable features twisted into a scowl.

"But how can I know it is me you want?" Henry asked. "How can I be certain of your affection?"

"You must be. I am here with you, am I not?"

"But were he here, you could say the same." Henry pulled his features into a ridiculous petulant look.

Anne wished he were a better actor.

"I approached you first, did I not?" Missy said with breathless urgency. "It has always been you, Henry. I only expressed affection for Richard once you turned me away." She pressed her palms to Henry's chest as she spoke, sliding her fingers under his coat. "He was a poor substitute for you, but I had to take what I could, to stay near to you. To be in your life."

Richard issued a gagging sound.

"Truly?" Henry asked.

"Truly." Missy slipped her hands free of Henry's coat, only to move them up to his neck. Coming up on her toes, she kissed him.

With a strangled, inarticulate yell, Richard burst from behind the apple trees. "What the devil is going on here?"

Her heels hitting the ground, Missy whirled and gasped, "Richard."

Anne shifted to ensure she was well hidden. This was between Richard and Missy now.

He stormed forward. "What do you mean, you always wanted Henry?"

Anne peeked to see Missy lift her chin defiantly. She took a step back, closer to Henry, and said, "I am sorry you had to find out this way, Richard, but I love your brother. I have always loved Henry and always will."

Henry snorted, his expression a mixture of amusement and disgust. "More like, you've always loved my title."

"And you." Richard turned to his brother. "How dare you plan an assignation with my intended?"

"Your intended?" Henry shook his head. "She cannot yet claim that honor, nor should she ever. I wanted you to see that before you got snared."

Missy's hands flew to her mouth as the import of Henry's words hit her. She turned from Richard to jab an accusatory finger into Henry's gut. "You never meant to offer for me. This was a trap. A cruel, heartless trap."

"Like the one you laid for my brother?" Henry cast back.

"Enough," Richard snapped. His words directed at Henry he said, "Brother or no, I should challenge you for this."

"For my honor?" Missy gasped, her face alight with hope while Anne's stomach gave a nauseated lurch.

She had not considered that Richard might challenge Henry. If they dueled, her father and Uncle Matlock really would send her to that horrible girls' school in Wales this time.

Richard turned back to her. "You have no honor, madam. Nor do you hold any place in my heart. Not from this day hence."

"I was only trying to help," Henry cut in. "I know a duplicitous tart when I see one and I could tell you do not."

"I am no such thing," Missy cried, red staining her cheeks. "Richard, my love, you cannot believe that of me."

Richard's hands fisted at his sides as he looked at her, then his brother. His anger so rigidly controlled that each word came out clipped and quiet, he said, "Out. Of. My. Sight."

"But Richard," Missy wailed even as Henry said, "I was only—"

"No." Richard's voice rang with rage. "No excuses. Go. Both of you."

Missy opened her mouth again, reaching out, but Richard stepped backward so she could not touch him.

"Go on," Henry muttered. "Go home, Missy, and be thankful we will never speak of this, so your reputation can remain intact."

Missy looked back and forth between the two brothers. She gave a little gasp, tears building in her eyes, whirled, and ran.

"I was only trying to help," Henry reiterated softly.

Richard merely glared at him.

Henry shrugged and strode off, head high. After a moment, he began to whistle, the cheery sound cutting back through the trees.

"You as well, Anne," Richard stated, not turning to face where she still hid. "Go. I wish for solitude."

Anne inched from behind the apple trees. "Henry and I wanted you to see her for who she really is before you threw your future away."

"I understand perfectly."

Anne could see little of Richard's face, his back almost full to her as he stood with his shoulders set and his hands balled, and asked, "Will you be well here on your own?"

"Better than I will be with you."

She winced and started to turn away.

"You had no right," Richard said softly.

Anne halted.

"No right to meddle in my happiness. Not you, or my father, or Henry."

"We have every right. We love you."

"Then you should have let me be happy."

Anne shook her head, though they did not face one another. "You would not have stayed happy. We could all see that."

"I believe I would have, and now I will never know."

A glance showed his head bowed, now. Anne pursed her lips. She did not want to leave him miserable and alone in the old orchard, but this was not her forte. This love nonsense.

She shrugged and left Richard to his grief, feeling unaccountably wretched as she strode back to the house. Missy had proved every bit as duplicitous as Anne feared. She and Henry had saved Richard from a lifetime with an awful, greedy person. And they'd done so out of love, with Anne's father's blessing, with not one hint of selfishness.

So why did Anne feel as if she'd done something terrible?

CHAPTER SEVEN

Anne tramped back to her chambers feeling quite glum, only to find Mrs. Jenkinson in the sitting room, reading. Looking up, her companion cocked her head slightly and asked, "Did you have an early hunt?"

Anne huffed a sigh and flopped down into a plush chair. "In a manner of speaking."

"Did it not go well?"

"Our quarry was caught."

"And yet you seem displeased."

Anne studied the other woman. Mrs. Jenkinson, Anne knew, was a skilled actor. She seemed politely curious, nothing more. But Anne knew her too well to believe that. "What do you know?"

Marking her place, Mrs. Jenkinson closed her book. "I know that your father asked you to intervene between Master Richard and Miss Steepleton. I know that Lord Henry left this house at an hour far earlier than he usually rises, let alone leaves his chambers, and that you departed shortly thereafter in the company of Master Richard." Mrs. Jenkinson pinned Anne with a severe look. "And I know that you should have discussed your hastily concocted plan with me before implementing it."

Anne sat up straighter. "It was not hastily concocted. It was a good plan, and it worked perfectly."

"Then why do you look as if you accidentally dropped your favorite rapier into the Thames?"

"Because Richard is terribly unhappy." Anne

leaned forward, in earnest now. "I thought he would be relieved. We showed him how horrible Missy is before he became engaged to her. Is that not grounds for relief? Perhaps even celebration?"

"My dear girl, you shattered his heart. Duplicitous or not, he loved her and now that love is dead. You killed it, as surely as if it were a pheasant."

"Oh." Anne sat back again, mulling over Mrs. Jenkinson's words. "But it had to be done. He couldn't be allowed to marry her."

"Could not," Mrs. Jenkinson corrected. "And I agree, their betrothal needed to be stopped, for both their good."

"Both?" Anne pulled a face. "Who cares about Missy's good? She was trapping Richard."

Mrs. Jenkinson regarded Anne with slightly raised eyebrows, clearly disappointed.

Anne crossed her arms over her chest and glared back.

"Well, if no one was physically harmed and the planned engagement is off, I suppose all is in order and I am certain that someday, once he is over his grief, Master Richard will thank you."

"He should thank me now," Anne muttered.

Ignoring that, Mrs. Jenkinson returned to her book.

Anne felt out of sorts all morning, no matter how many times she thought about having done the right thing. Richard did not take any meals with the family that day, if he took any at all, or join them after dinner. That was likely fortunate as their evening conversation revolved around Uncle Matlock's news that Richard had rescinded his request to become engaged to Missy.

Anne woke the next morning feeling much better.

She had, after all, done right by Richard, and even Mrs. Jenkinson agreed that he would be thankful someday. Anne would simply wait until that day, and then extract an apology from him for being so horrid about her saving him from a lifetime of misery.

Her good cheer restored, she breakfasted and then sought Richard. Now that he needn't work at getting ordained, he would be free for a ride, or perhaps even a hunt, or to practice shooting.

Directed by the staff, she eventually found him in the library, right back at the table he'd been using, surrounded by the same books. Leeriness washing through her, she strode up to the table to demand, "What are you doing? I thought the intended betrothal was no longer intended?"

Richard looked up with a frown. "Yes, but I am still pursuing a life in the church."

Anne stared at him, aghast. "You cannot mean that. You've always wanted to be an officer. Always."

Richard shook his head, sorrow darkening his eyes. "I am not suited to lead others into battle. Look at how terribly I misjudged Miss Steepleton. How easily she fooled me. I am obviously not a man upon whom other men can depend to make the right decisions, and in war, those decisions don't simply mean an unhappy marriage. They mean men's lives."

Anger shot through Anne. "You were born to be an officer, Richard. Anyone can see that. You cannot let one error in judgment dictate your future."

"But I did. My error in believing in Miss Steepleton's affections would have dictated my future if you and Henry had not intervened. On the field of battle, no one will be there to set me straight." He met her gaze and cleared his throat. "And I owe you thanks. I appreciate that you risked my ire in order to help me."

He said it so glumly, so formally, that Anne found no satisfaction in the words. "I didn't do it to get your thanks," she snapped, trying not to dwell on how she'd wanted just that yesterday. "I did it to make certain you have the future you should."

"And I will. In the church." Richard let out a long sigh. "It is a shame, though. All those years of working hard at riding and shooting. I truly did want to serve King and Country."

"Then you should," Anne cried.

He shook his head. "No. I am more suited to the priesthood, it seems. My father was right, and you and I were wrong. That is all there is to it." With that, Richard dropped his gaze back to his papers and books.

Uncle Matlock right and her wrong? Not very likely. Anne glared at Richard, but he didn't look back up. Finally, she marched from the library.

Apparently, she was not yet done saving Richard from his own folly, but she wouldn't give up. She simply needed a new plan.

CHAPTER EIGHT

After leaving the library, Anne went to her sitting room to pace, ideas roiling in her mind. Each rose to the surface and popped, like air bubbling up through porridge. As each one exploded, useless, new ones formed.

Mrs. Jenkinson entered, book in hand. She halted to watch Anne pace for a moment, then moved to sit in her favorite chair. Opening her book to the marked page, she observed, "You seem agitated. Has this to do with Master Richard's insistence on joining the priesthood even after you and Lord Henry enacted your trap?"

"What else would it have to do with?" Anne demanded, whirling to pace back across the room. "He's being an utter fool."

"You do realize that men trained to the priesthood may still join the regulars? He is only seventeen. He has time to change his mind."

"Henry and I didn't expose Missy so that Richard would keep on with this ridiculous plan to be ordained."

"Did not," Mrs. Jenkinson corrected. "And I believe you missed the salient point of my statement."

"I can fix this," Anne said, ignoring her. "I can restore Richard's confidence. Remind him that he is a man of action, not reflection."

"Can he not be both?"

Anne halted to cast her companion an incredulous look. "Certainly not. There are men of action like

Richard, and men who think and think about everything, like Darcy. Now, were Darcy a second son, I wouldn't discourage him from joining the church one bit. He could give all sorts of boring, sensible advice and drone on every Sunday about right and wrong. He would be sublimely happy." She resumed her pacing.

"Have you ever entertained the idea that perhaps you should not be meddling in people's lives this way?" Mrs. Jenkinson asked from her chair. "That you may not even have the right?"

Anne scrunched her nose as she paced, thinking that over. Finally, she shook her head. "No. I will be mistress of Rosings someday. Ordering people's lives is what I will do, day in and day out, to ensure that those beholden to me have the best lives possible."

"Be that as it may, you will be overseeing your holdings. Your concerns will be on a broad scale. Plantings, roads, bridges, and the like. You will not, for example, dictate who can marry whom."

"I will if I see someone about to make a terrible mistake," Anne countered. "A good landholder takes a keen interest in the lives of their tenants."

"Master Richard is your cousin, not your tenant."

Anne waved that off. "He requires my assistance to put his life back right. I won't help only my tenants when I am mistress of Rosings, but anyone who requires my help."

"I see." Mrs. Jenkinson dropped her gaze to her book. "And what, precisely, do you intend to do this time?"

Not halting her agitated stride, Anne narrowed her eyes, studying her companion. She couldn't let Mrs. Jenkinson ruin whatever plan she came up with. "I have not yet decided."

"Hmm," Mrs. Jenkinson murmured, giving every appearance of disinterest as she began to read. "Well, if you would like to discuss your plans, I am always here."

Anne held in a snort. Discuss her plans indeed. She would not. Not even the one now welling up in her mind. She mentally prodded at it, and it didn't explode. Halting, she said, "I would like to call on Miss Steepleton again, to offer my friendship. Maybe that will be some comfort to her in the wake of Richard's change of mind."

Mrs. Jenkinson raised a calm gaze. "Will this afternoon be soon enough?"

Matching her companion's unconcern, Anne shrugged. "Certainly. I am in no hurry." She made a show of turning to the mantel clock to check the time. "For now, I believe I will go for a ride." All innocence, she added, "Would you care to join me?"

"I am certain a groom will be company enough. You know I do not care for the equine."

"Very well. Until luncheon, then."

"Have a pleasant ride," Mrs. Jenkinson responded.

With a nod, Anne went to change.

She did ride, wanting the clean, open air to work out the details of her plan. She also wished to inspect the old tenant's cottage on the other side of the duck pond, the side near where the Steepletons lived. Reaching it, she was pleased to find it vacant but mostly intact. The shuttered windows and slightly ajar but functional door were perfect for her plan. Anne grinned as she remounted her horse under the watchful eye of her accompanying groom. Turning the gelding, she set out for her uncle's house.

She dressed with care that afternoon, striving for a look of even competence. It would be difficult to convince Missy to be a part of her plan, so Anne wanted to appear very reliable. Hopefully that would help, as well, with crafting a means of speaking with the other young lady alone. Anne certainly couldn't impart her idea with Mrs. Jenkinson and Missy's mother listening.

To that end, Anne waited until the carriage slowed near the parsonage to adopt a thoughtful expression and say, "Do you know, I believe it would be good if I could speak to Missy with some privacy. She may be more frank in her feelings away from her mother's ear, and once she is frank, I will be better able to offer sympathy."

"If you feel that is best," Mrs. Jenkinson said with a mildness that Anne didn't trust.

They were shown into the same drawing room as before, but this time, while Mrs. Steepleton appeared no different, Missy slumped in her place on the sofa. She rose slowly to greet them, her shoulders drooping and her gaze downcast. A pang of guilt hit Anne, but she pushed it aside as greetings were exchanged and they all sat.

"Would you care for tea, Miss de Bourgh, Mrs. Jenkinson?" Mrs. Steepleton asked.

"That would be pleasant, thank you," Anne replied.

Mrs. Steepleton nodded to the waiting maid, then turned back to say, "It is lovely weather we're having, is it not?"

"Truly." Anne looked about the room. Could she ask to see the same paintings again? Would that afford her and Missy enough privacy for Anne to broach her plan?

"So lovely, in fact, that I believe we should encourage the young people to have a stroll before tea," Mrs. Jenkinson said. She aimed a commiserative smile at Missy. "If I am not being too bold, Miss Steepleton, you appear as if fresh air may enliven you."

Mrs. Steepleton cast her daughter a quick look and frowned. "Mrs. Jenkinson is correct, dear. You are positively dreary."

"I would be pleased to walk with you," Anne offered. She may not trust Mrs. Jenkinson wanting to help, but she would certainly take the opportunity provided.

Missy shrugged, standing. Without a word she turned and started from the room.

Anne hastened to follow, but did not speak until they were safely in the garden, strolling a well-tended path. Finally, deeming that they were far enough from the parsonage to go unheard, she opened her mouth.

"He hates me now, doesn't he?" Missy blurted before Anne could speak.

Out of the corner of her eye, Anne took in the misery on Missy's face. "Well, I do not think he likes you, at least."

Missy let out a gusty sigh. "I was so close. I should have known Henry's invitation was false. He turned me down in no uncertain terms when last I made my inclination known to him."

Inclination known? Did Missy care for Henry in truth?

Halting, Missy brought Anne up short as she turned to face her. "You delivered Lord Henry's message." Missy scrutinized Anne through narrowed eyes. "Did you know Richard would spy on us?"

Anne hated to lie when she didn't have to, so instead she asked, "Does it matter?"

Missy let out a long breath, slumping. "I do not suppose it does." She raised beseeching eyes to Anne. "What will I do now? I will never have a season. My father's refusal of that is what drove me to try for Lord Henry and Richard in the first place."

"There must be someone else you could..." Anne trailed off, for all the words she thought of smacked of condemnation.

Missy was shaking her head. "Living on the earl's land, we have little access to society with young, eligible men. I will die a spinster."

"You're sixteen," Anne protested, for Missy was only one year her senior. "You have years to find a husband."

"Two, maybe three," Missy muttered glumly.

"Are you certain you even need one?" Anne snapped, angered by the other young woman's self-pity.

Missy gaped at her as if Anne were mad. "Yes, I need one. What would I be without a husband? Some . . . some nanny somewhere? To a family who could not afford a real nanny?"

"I don't know," Anne admitted. She had Rosings, after all, whether she married or not. She didn't know what women who didn't marry and had no fortune were driven to. To what fate she may have consigned Missy.

She would have to ask Henry.

Missy moaned. "I am doomed."

Anne's anger sparked again. "Do not be absurd." She jabbed a finger at Missy. "You are young, educated, intelligent. You need to have real goals, not squander all you are by latching onto the first man who will have you." Even if Richard was worth latching onto, insofar as such things went. "You need to be strong and to ask what you want from your life, not what your father and mother want for you, and to formulate dreams and work to bring them to fruition. You are hobbling yourself, when you should be taking actions on your behalf."

"But—" Missy began.

Speaking over her, Anne continued, "Yes, you will almost certainly end up married to some man, being his wife and making his heir, but do so on your terms, with a man of your choosing. Act out of strength and certainty, not fear."

Her mouth hinged open in shock, Missy stared as if Anne had grown two heads.

Anne sucked in a breath, aware that she'd gone off track, railing against the failings of their world rather than pursuing her goal for Richard.

"M-my own dreams?" Missy stammered.

Anne nodded sharply. "Yes. Your own dreams."

Missy dropped her gaze to the gravel path, blinking rapidly. When she looked up again, it was to glare at Anne through narrowed eyes. "What do you want from me? Why did your companion suggest we walk alone?"

"She suggested as much because I'd said I wished to offer my sympathies in private, out of hearing of your mother."

"And why did you truly want to speak with me alone?"

Anne smiled, pleased to see Missy thinking, rather than wallowing. "Because I need your help to help Richard."

Missy's brows drew down into a vee. "My help? He will not want it and I cannot see why I should give it."

"You should give it because you wronged him and you know it. This will make amends. And as to if he wants it, that doesn't signify. He needs it."

Missy huffed, but nodded. "What help can I be?"

"I need a lock of your hair, and for you to go tomorrow to that empty tenant's house near the duck pond, alone."

Missy shook her head. "My mother knows that what transpired in the orchard ended my almost-engagement, though I merely told her that Richard and I had a disagreement. I doubt she will ever permit me to walk out alone again."

"So sneak out," Anne said impatiently.

"Why do you want me to be in that cottage alone?"

"Richard is a man of action who needs his confidence restored, so we will create the opportunity for him to take action."

"That explains nothing," Missy noted, her hands finding her hips. "Tell me your plan or I won't help."

Anne glared at her, but could only respect her resolve. "It's not general knowledge yet that your agreement is broken. So, before it is, we're going to stage a kidnapping, as if someone has taken you to get to him. You'll go to the cottage and pretend to be tied up, and I'll take your hair and make a fake ransom note. He'll come save you, because he's Richard, and he'll succeed because there aren't any kidnappers, anyhow."

"But . . . won't he want to find them?"

Anne shrugged, having not quite worked that out yet. "You'll say they got worried and decided to flee to Ireland or some such. Just make certain you say their faces were covered so Richard cannot ask you to describe them."

"I do not know. This sounds as if it could go very wrong." Missy pursed her lips, appearing deep in thought. "What if Richard wants to go to my father, or his?"

"If things go that far I will confess. I can even say I tricked you into going there, if you like."

"You will be in terrible trouble," Missy said nervously.

Anne shrugged. "I'm in trouble a great deal. Once more won't really matter."

Missy dropped her gaze again, her features pinched in thought. "You truly believe this will help Richard? I do feel dreadful about what he overheard, and it wasn't even true. He's far kinder than Henry. I'd much rather be married to Richard."

It was Anne's turn to frown. "Then why did you leap at the opportunity to be with Henry?"

In a miserable whisper, Missy admitted, "Because all I could think of was how wonderful it would be to be the wife of an earl, and of getting to tell my father that I would be. And, well, marrying a peer is what every woman wants, is it not?"

"Is it what *you* want?" Anne said pointedly.

Missy shook her head. "I do not even know. I've never thought about it." She lifted her gaze, studying the sky somewhere above Anne's left shoulder.

Silence stretched between them.

Finally, annoyed, Anne asked, "So will you help me or not?"

Missy met her gaze squarely. "I will help you."

A grin stretched Anne's face. "Perfect." She pulled out her penknife. "Now, for your hair."

She secured a lock from the back of Missy's head where it wouldn't be missed, and Missy even supplied a piece of one of her ribbons, which did not cut well with the penknife. They then talked for a short time more, working out details and picking a time for Richard's so-called rescue to take place. Anne agreed again that if their plan turned into trouble, she would take the blame, and then they returned to have tea.

Anne devoured several small cakes and tarts, and chatted about the parsonage garden and Missy's skill with watercolors, quite satisfied with the outing. Missy seemed more cheerful as well and her mother looked pleased by the change. Soon enough, Anne and Mrs. Jenkinson rose to go.

They were nearly to the carriage when Mrs. Jenkinson halted. "Why, I seem to have left my shawl. How careless of me. I won't be a moment." Turning, she went back to the house.

Anne climbed into the carriage, her mind more on her plan than on Mrs. Jenkinson or shawls. She fingered the lock of Missy's hair. With that, and the note she would craft, Richard's natural inclination to heroism would take over and soon he would be put right.

And then he would once more have to thank her.

CHAPTER NINE

Later that afternoon found Anne tiptoeing along a bare corridor, dimly lit by a single window in the center and blessedly empty. Having been party to many a pilfering over the years with her cousins Richard and Darcy, Anne knew that Uncle Matlock's old housekeeper, Mrs. Penn, napped after tea and before dinner preparations became hectic. The rest of the staff knew this as well and took just as much advantage of the lack of oversight as Anne and her cousins routinely did.

Unlike usual, Anne didn't seek sweets or other victuals, or linens for forts, something they'd been fiercely reprimanded for. She simply sought paper. Normal, unadorned, middling quality paper, and Mrs. Penn kept a supply in her office for the staff.

As she neared the end of the corridor, Anne sighted her goal, the housekeeper's office. She slipped her lockpicks from her skirt pocket.

She'd been practicing picking locks for some years now and was proficient, but not yet quick about it. It would be deuced difficult to explain were she caught in the act, so she paused to listen intently. Then, feeling a touch silly for not doing so immediately, she tried the door.

It opened and Anne grinned, sliding the lockpicks back into her pocket. It was a good thing her cousins weren't there to see her nearly waste time picking an already unlocked lock. She slipped into the office and took a piece of paper. Then, after a little thought, took several more. She only required one but she was prone to errors.

Or did kidnappers not care if their ransom notes were well written?

Leaving the scene of her pilfering while mulling that over, Anne set out down the corridor. She hurried, not wanting any witnesses to her presence, pages in hand, in case Mrs. Penn kept careful enough track to realize that some were missing, which she very well might. Anne also wanted to get to her room before her companion could appear.

Mrs. Jenkinson, too, had decided to nap after tea. Anne had waited as long as she dared, listening at Mrs. Jenkinson's door to ensure that she truly was resting, but eventually haste had overcome caution and Anne had given up her spying to come steal the paper. Napping wasn't a usual occupation for Anne's companion and so may not last long, and Mrs. Penn's naps ended very predictably on the hour.

As she passed the lone window that lighted the long servants' corridor, movement without caught Anne's eye. Pausing, she sighted Mrs. Jenkinson, very assuredly not napping, speaking to a cloaked and hooded figure. The figure, whose height and slender build suggested a woman though Anne couldn't see a face, dipped her head and turned away. Mrs. Jenkinson watched her go.

Then Mrs. Jenkinson's shoulders tensed. Her head tipped up like a sparrow taking note of the presence of a person. She turned searching eyes on the house.

But Anne was already moving away from the window, frowning. What was Mrs. Jenkinson doing in the garden? Who was under that cloak?

And how did Mrs. Jenkinson always seem to know

when Anne was doing something nefarious?

Worried her companion would enter the house and go directly to check on her, Anne rushed back to her chambers and hid the pilfered pages in the desk in her bedroom. She then returned to her sitting room and grabbed a book. Flopping down into an armchair with the book open in her lap, she concentrated on slowing her breathing to a normal, not suspicious rate.

The door to her sitting room opened and she looked up to see Mrs. Jenkinson come in. As Mrs. Jenkinson turned to close the door behind her, Anne noticed she had the book the wrong way around and quickly turned it the right way up.

Her smile of greeting innocent, Anne asked, "How was your nap?"

"Short." Mrs. Jenkinson crossed to take her usual place near the fire. "I was interrupted by a maid."

"Whyever for?"

"It was a personal matter. An inquiry for advice." Mrs. Jenkinson shook her head. "There is a dearth of sympathetic, seasoned female ears here."

"There's Mrs. Penn." And the older maids, but if one of the younger ones desired advice, they may not have wanted to go to their direct superiors with the matter.

"True enough," Mrs. Jenkinson acknowledged and reached for her sewing.

"Do you know," Anne said lightly, closing the book and standing, "I have a letter I would like to finish before dinner, if you will excuse me."

Mrs. Jenkinson looked up from her sewing basket. "Excuse you? But there is a desk right there." She nodded to an elegant piece of furniture set before one of the room's two tall windows.

"Yes, but there is one in my bedchamber as well, and all of my writing things are already atop it."

"You could bring them in here easily enough, to keep me company."

Anne narrowed her eyes. Did Mrs. Jenkinson want the opportunity to see her letter? "But I require quiet to compose." And she needed Mrs. Jenkinson not to be spying over her shoulder as she worked out how to make her handwriting appear not to be her own, which Richard would recognize as surely as he would have her stationary.

"I see you are reading about Persephone," Mrs. Jenkinson observed rather than replying to Anne's words, her gaze dropping to the book Anne held. "An interesting choice. An instance, I believe, of Zeus's interference in the lives of others doing good. Likely not the best example for you to follow."

Anne fought down a flush. Of all the books she and Mrs. Jenkinson had accumulated in their room so far during their visit, why had she inadvertently picked up one of the world's most well-known tales of kidnapping? "I was merely passing the time while you rested. Which you were not," Anne added, deciding the time had come to turn the tables. If Mrs. Jenkinson suspected something, then so did she. "You were giving advice, which I daresay is simply a more amiable way of saying interfering."

"I was giving solicited advice, which is far more like offering aid."

"Sometimes people cannot see that they require aid, and so cannot solicit it," Anne said primly. "Now, if you will excuse me." She pivoted and left the room, closing her bedchamber door firmly behind her.

CHAPTER TEN

It had taken Anne many sheets of her own stationary before she felt confident in her kidnapper's handwriting, but by morning she had a ransom note on paper that could not be readily linked to her. Hardly able to contain her delight that soon her plan would unfold, she breakfasted with her father, who seemed a bit grouchy, a cheerful Uncle Matlock, and Mrs. Jenkinson. Henry, of course, was not yet awake, and Richard had already ensconced himself in the library.

Later in the morning, having told Mrs. Jenkinson that she would be in the library with Richard, Anne sneaked into a little used parlor near the front of the house. The door cracked open, she spent an aggravating forty-odd minutes peeking out, awaiting the daily missives. Finally a footman arrived and placed them on the salver that rested on a narrow table near the front door.

Before her uncle's ever-efficient butler could appear, Anne stepped out and went to the letters, then pretended to leaf through them as she slipped the note bearing Richard's name into the pile. A quick glance showed no one about, meaning no one could have seen her add the note. Satisfied that the butler would distribute the mail soon, she hurried to the library.

She stepped in, slightly fearful that an accusatory Mrs. Jenkinson would be waiting, but found only her cousin. She crossed to his cluttered table, taking in books on philosophy and doctrine. "Good morning, Richard. How go your studies?"

He looked up, suspicion clear on his face. "I assume you do not actually care and only wish to find footing for an argument against my chosen course?"

"Me? Argue?" Anne asked, wide-eyed. "Am I to take it that means your studies do not progress well?"

"You see? Even when I give you no indication of my progress, you find a means by which to argue."

Anne adopted a slightly hurt expression. "You wound me, sir." Turning, she spotted a chair and dragged it over so she could sit opposite him. "Tell me all about your deeply fascinating delve into church doctrine."

He sat back to contemplate her. "Much of it is quite interesting, you know. I can now far better appreciate the care and subtlety that goes into a Sunday sermon."

Anne waited but he said no more, simply regarded her, so she pressed, "But?"

Richard set aside his pen to scrub both hands over his face. Dropping them to the tabletop he admitted, "I feel no passion for it."

Anne leaned forward. "Then abandon this silliness and return to your pursuit of a commission."

His jaw jutting slightly, he shook his head. "No. I will not be so fickle. Nor have I changed my mind about my ability to lead."

Footsteps in the hall cut off Anne's launch into her 'man of action' speech and they both turned to see the butler enter. "Master Fitzwilliam, Miss de Bourgh," he greeted as he reached them, proffering his tray.

"Thank you," Anne and Richard chorused.

Anne took up her letter, from Darcy of course. As they were eventually-to-be-betrothed, he took writing to her regularly very seriously. Although she could already guess everything Darcy would have to say, that being a detailed report of each day since his previous letter the week before, in which none of the days would differ from usual, Anne made a show of starting to open the letter. In truth, her concentration was on Richard, who sorted through his three missives as the butler departed.

"What is this?"

Anne turned her full attention on Richard, making certain her eyes were wide and devoid of excitement at her plan going into action. "What is what?"

Richard looked up from the plain page, his expression a mixture of shock and anger. "This. It says that Miss Steepleton has been taken and will only be handed over safely if I bring fifty pounds to that old cottage by the duck pond."

"What?" Anne gasped. "Surely, that cannot be true. We would have heard were she missing."

His expression grave, Richard held up the lock of hair, tied with one of Missy's pink ribbons. "This is her hair. I know it is. I recognize the precise color and the ribbon."

"What will you do?" Anne gasped. "Go to your father?"

Richard shook his head. "It says in the note that if I do, the kidnappers will know and they will take her somewhere far less hospitable and abandon her."

Anne had to struggle not to grin, being quite pleased with that part. "How horrible."

Richard came to his feet. "I have thirty-five pounds. Do you have any, Anne?"

"You are going to pay them?" She hadn't expected that. Richard was meant to rescue Missy, an easy task as he would find her alone, the kidnappers having mysteriously vanished.

"I'm not certain. I will take the ransom with me, though. If I can use it to ensure her safety, then I will." His expression very grave, Richard added, "Getting her back safe is what is most important."

Anne stood as well but asked, "Not taking vengeance on whoever took her?" That's what she would have found most important.

Richard shook his head. "Do you have fifteen pounds or not?"

"I do. I'll get it and meet you in the stable."

"You aren't to come with me. This is serious."

"So am I," Anne said primly and turned to stride across the room so he could argue no further.

She left, as well, because she could no longer suppress a grin. Her plan was working perfectly. Next, they would gallop to the cottage. Richard would rush in and find Missy, untie her and save her, and be a hero.

He would realize he was meant for action, not contemplation, and tell his father that he would become an officer after all. Maybe he would even forgive Missy, while still realizing she wasn't for him, and she would not have to live with the guilt that she'd ruined his dreams. Everyone would end up happy, all thanks to Anne.

Yes. Everything was going to plan.

CHAPTER ELEVEN

They did gallop, Richard pushing his mount hard enough that Anne had to concentrate on her riding to keep up. When they drew near, he pulled up and they dismounted, leaving their horses tethered to a tree as they inched forward through a scraggly copse. Richard stalked with intensity and purpose and Anne, ducking her head to hide the expression, permitted another grin.

They drew in sight of the cottage and dropped down to crouch in the tangled brush at the edge of the copse. Richard scanned the area before them, calm and focused.

Without looking at her he said, "You go around the back. We can't know if they have mounts there. We can't permit them to escape once we have Missy."

"What will you do?" Anne asked quietly, so pleased to hear Richard give an order that she didn't even take offense that he'd issued it to her.

He pulled a pistol from under his coat. "I'm going in the front. I've decided these miscreants cannot have our fifty pounds."

"Put that away," Anne hissed, not liking the idea of him bursting in on Missy with a gun.

"It will be dark in there after all this daylight," he said, ignoring her. "So don't follow me. I wouldn't want to shoot you by mistake."

"Don't shoot anyone," Anne snapped.

But Richard was already moving.

Anne rushed after him as he ran for the cottage,

pistol cocked and held out before him at the ready, his long legs propelling him faster than she could go. Richard plowed in, sending the door flying.

Anne yelled, "Don't shoot anybody," and ran harder.

A feminine scream sounded, and a report, loud even though it was contained in the cracked stone dwelling.

"Oh no, what have I done?" Richard's voice cried inside the cottage. "There's so much blood. Missy, don't die!"

Her heart thudding madly, Anne flung through the cottage doorway.

To the sight of Missy, Richard, and Mrs. Jenkinson standing in a row, waiting for her.

Anne gaped at them.

Missy lowered the hands she had clamped over her ears. Richard grinned, stowing his pistol. Mrs. Jenkinson regarded Anne with the barest hint of a smile.

The frantic race of Anne's heart slowed. She pressed her mouth into a hard line, then opened it to say, "If I had died of shock, you would not find this so amusing."

"You are young and hale. There was little danger of that," Mrs. Jenkinson replied.

"So we did scare you?" Missy asked.

Anne scowled at her.

"We terrified her," Richard chortled.

"Good," Missy said with a sniff. "Because it was an awfully mean thing, setting me up with Lord Henry."

Anne deepened her scowl. "It was an awfully mean thing to try to trap Richard into a loveless union and an occupation not suited to him."

Missy sighed, pique draining from her. "I know, and I am sorry." She turned to Richard. "Truly, I am. I did believe that we would have come to love one another, though, you being as good and kind as you are."

He looked down at her with a tenderness Anne couldn't like. "And perhaps someday we still will, Miss Steepleton, once we are both older. I cannot speak for you, but I believe I need to live a bit more before I marry."

To Anne's surprise, Missy smiled. "I wholeheartedly agree. I have many years left to marry. First, I need to discover what it is I want in a gentleman, and maybe even in life. There must be more than painting watercolors." She lay a hand along his cheek. "Thank you."

"So you all colluded against me, then?" Anne asked, aware of petulance in her voice but unable to suppress it. She glared at Mrs. Jenkinson. "I imagine this was your plan, to teach me not to meddle in people's lives."

"Certainly, though I have strong doubts about your ability to absorb the lesson."

Anne studied her companion for a long moment, then turned her dour expression on the other two, thoroughly put out. "You are all very pleased with yourselves, aren't you?"

Richard's grin returned. "You should have seen your face, de Bourgh. I thought you would keel over on the spot."

"It is good to know that you would care if I were shot," Missy added.

"We should have had you play dead," Richard said to Missy. "Then we would know if she would help me bury the body."

"You know I would have," Anne snapped, but her ire was already beginning to melt. They'd fooled her, fair and square. If she'd pulled the prank, she would be delighted. Still, she couldn't help but mutter, "I will get even, you know."

"And yet, the look on your face was still worth it," Richard answered, though Missy appeared slightly uneasy at the threat.

Mrs. Jenkinson, of course, remained serene, merely saying, "I will escort Miss Steepleton home. Her mother believes we are walking together."

"Which we did and will," Missy said quickly.

Mrs. Jenkinson nodded.

"Come on, de Bourgh." Richard strode forward with a cheerful grin. "Let's get our horses. On the ride back, I can tell you all about how I'd already concluded that the church wasn't for me even before Mrs. Jenkinson recruited me to teach you a lesson."

"Certainly," Anne said with as much grace as she could muster. She dipped her head to Mrs. Jenkinson and Missy. "Enjoy your walk."

"Thank you," Missy murmured, still appearing a touch leery.

Richard bid the two farewell as well, then joined Anne in leaving the cottage. As they crossed back to the copse, Anne said, "You owe me fifteen pounds."

Richard shook his head. "Payment for my suffering."

"Your suffering? I'm the one who nearly keeled over."

"As Mrs. Jenkinson said, you're too hearty to do that, de Bourgh." Richard cast her a quick, gleeful look. "But let's say that when we reach the open ground at the end of the eastern briar patch, we race the rest of the way to the stable. Winner gets the fifteen pounds."

"If you win, you get my fifteen. If I win, I get mine and fifteen of yours," Anne countered.

"Deal," Richard said, pressing into the brush at the edge of the copse.

Anne followed with a grin of her own. Yes, they'd tricked her quite thoroughly and yes, she'd had a shock she would not easily forget, but soon she would have fifteen pounds of her cousin's money to make up for it all. On top of that, her father would be pleased that Richard once again planned to follow his heart into service to the Crown, and she truly had learned a lesson.

And that lesson was that next time, she had to be sneakier, especially when it came to Mrs. Jenkinson.

This adventure of Miss Anne de Bourgh's is a *Pride & Prejudice* variation prequel to *Mr. Darcy's Bookshop*, a Darcy and Elizabeth centered love story. I hope you enjoyed reading!

For a sneak peek of *Mr. Darcy's Bookshop*, read on…

Mr. Darcy's Bookshop

by

Summer Hanford

CHAPTER ONE

November, 1811

Fitzwilliam Darcy pushed his spectacles up on his nose, for they were forever slipping. A more finely crafted pair might better remain in place, but could he afford those, he would need none, for he would be back in Pemberley with more activities at hand than going over his shop records by tallow light. At Pemberley, he would read during the day, for pleasure, with bright sunlight streaming into finely furnished rooms. And if he wrote, there would be no need for cramped letters he could hardly make out, simply to save on watery ink and coarse paper.

Finishing with his records for the day, he snuffed out all the tallow candles but one, then carefully trimmed down the wicks. Rising from the counter at the front of the bookshop, he took the remaining candle and made a check of the doors, front and back, though why anyone would want to rob a bookseller he didn't know. Satisfied his wares were safe for the night, he took the cashbox and went up the back stairs to the room above, where he finished the watered ale and half-eaten hand pie he'd procured earlier that day.

Going to the other side of the room, he readied for bed, then blew out the candle. By memory and feel, he crossed back to his narrow cot and climbed beneath thin sheets. So far, November had been mild, but soon enough London would grow cold and cloaked in a smoky miasma, and Darcy would shiver in his sleep. Perhaps if he went to his cousin Richard...but no. He wouldn't put Richard in the position of being at odds with the patriarchs.

Darcy sought rest, his mind on books and ledgers and the price of tallow. It did not help that he had sold only a single volume today, most of which had been spent dusting to keep the shop in good order and to give him something to do. Nor was tomorrow likely to be much different, although soon patrons would trickle in, seeking gifts to take back to their country estates for the Yuletide. December would be a better month. It always had been in years past.

He listened to the light patter of rain on the eaves,

well aware he would face the same worries on the morrow. And the next day, and the following. Every day would be thus, until he relented to his father's and uncles' command that he marry his cousin Anne de Bourgh. Though he certainly wished no harm to his kin, no matter how they tormented, sometimes Darcy liked to imagine how his circumstances would differ had his father, Matlock, and Sir Lewis had died when he was young, rather than his mother and his aunts. Surely, as a mother, Lady Catherine would have laid to rest this nonsense about Darcy and Anne marrying. Were she alive still, Anne would be happily wedded already, and Darcy would be free from his imagined obligation to espouse her. He was certain of it.

Darcy drifted off during his wistful musings, to wake cold and stiff shortly before dawn. He dressed for the day then stoked his small stove to heat water for tea, which he brewed in a chipped pot. The precious leaves and the heat to boil water for them were the one luxury he wouldn't do without, his morning cup far more important than a second blanket.

Later, down in the shop, he unlocked the front door and put out the sign, then returned to his dusting. He began with the low, chest-height shelving at the front of the shop, then moved on to the taller shelves in the back of the store. Dust and disorderliness, he'd found, were the greatest enemies of a bookshop, aside from a lack of patrons. Immersed in his work, he didn't consider that it was the third Monday of the month until much later when the front door opened, the bell jangling, to admit George Wickham.

Darcy started to scowl, then mastered the expression as a second man entered on Wickham's heels. An amiable looking fellow in his early twenties, with neither great height nor over-fine looks to distinguish him, but a cheerful air of affability. By his garb and his presence with Wickham, Darcy assumed him to be wealthy. Wickham had no use for companions he couldn't count on to foot the bills, no matter how much money Darcy's father showered him with.

"Darcy," Wickham greeted with false warmth, sauntering over to the short ladder on which Darcy stood to reach the highest shelves. "Hard at work, I see. Come down here and I'll introduce you."

Leaving the feather duster on the shelf, Darcy climbed down the ladder. He pulled out a handkerchief to wipe his hands.

"Bingley, may I present an old friend of mine, Fitzwilliam Darcy?" Wickham turned back to Darcy. "And this is Mr. Charles Bingley."

"Pleased to make your acquaintance," Mr. Bingley said affably. "Darcy? Isn't that the name of your patron, Wickham? Any relation? I hear the Darcys are quite the thing in Derbyshire."

"Why yes, Fitz here is somewhat related to the Darcys in Derbyshire," Wickham said. He eyed Darcy sardonically and added, "He's a poor relation, though, to be certain. I come by once a month to check on him."

"Too good of you," Mr. Bingley said, looking about. "Fine shop you have here, Darcy."

"Thank you."

"Quite a lot of books, isn't it?" Mr. Bingley continued. "I wish my collection were larger, but I am an idle fellow, and though I have not many, I have more than I ever look into. Still, can't hurt to browse."

"You do that," Wickham said. "Darcy and I are due a chat."

"Books on horseflesh and fencing are up front on those back two shelves there," Darcy added, pointing to the front corner of the shop.

"Excellent," Mr. Bingley said and wandered in that direction.

Darcy turned to Wickham. "My father won't approve of you bringing me a customer."

"Bingley?" Wickham raised his eyebrows. "You heard him. He's not the reading sort. He's having a devil of a time at university."

"Is that where you found him? Haven't you finished at university yet?"

Wickham shrugged. "I recently decided to give law a go. Had to start all over. Your father was more than happy to sell off that living he wanted me to fill and give me the funds to further my education."

Darcy eyed the loathsome being before him and wondered how much money Wickham had swindled from George Darcy this time.

"Five thousand," Wickham said, following Darcy's thoughts, for they knew each other well, having been raised nearly as brothers. "The living didn't go for that much but my dear, dear godfather wanted to ensure I am comfortable while at my studies, so he augmented the sum." Wickham leaned near, lowering his voice to say, "By the time you give up this ridiculous show of independence, you'll be begging to marry your hoyden of a cousin just to refill Pemberley's coffers, the way your father spends money on me."

"Anne is not a hoyden." Not that anything about Anne was why Darcy would never relent to his father's demand that they wed. They simply did not suit, and being cut off from his family's money wouldn't persuade Darcy that they did. He would never give in to his father's tyranny.

"Of course she is," Wickham countered. "She rides and hunts and shoots. I've only ever seen her in boots and a habit, a crop in hand. Your uncle raised her to be the son his late wife didn't give him, which is why I sympathize with you not wanting to wed her, but you'll get Rosings, man. Stop this ridiculous charade and get the banns read."

"Must we do this every third Monday?" Darcy asked. "I have dusting to do."

Wickham shook his head. "Who would have thought, back at Eton, that the great Fitzwilliam Darcy of Pemberley would spend his days dusting piles of worthless books."

"I take exception to the notion that books are worthless."

"Do you?" Wickham shrugged again. "Never found a single one I liked. Well, not here. You don't stock any of those bawdy ones with the pictures that they bring back from India."

"No," Darcy said coldly. "I do not. This is a respectable establishment."

"This? Only by dint of you being here. We're in Cheapside, after all. It's a stone's throw to the grand import warehouses."

"Did you say import warehouses?" Mr. Bingley said, striding over with three books in hand. "Fine places, those. Always trying to convince my sisters to get their fabrics and feathers and whatnots there. All the modistes do. Why pay for the markup, I say."

Darcy agreed. The great open-air market in the center of the warehouse district was where he made many of his purchases, including his tea.

Wickham chuckled. "My dear fellow, you pay for the markup so everyone will know that you can afford to." He shook his head, his charming countenance molded into amusement, with just a touch of condescension. "How about you treat me to lunch and I'll expound on the subject for you? You have a lot to learn if you wish to properly disentangle from your roots in trade."

Mr. Bingley pulled a face. "Don't I know it. My sisters are constantly on about the same thing."

"Well, if there's anyone who can educate you on how to best employ money to appear every inch the gentleman, it's me." Wickham cocked an eyebrow at Darcy. "Wouldn't you agree, Darcy?"

"Yes," Darcy said dryly. "On that, Mr. Wickham and I can very much agree."

"Splendid," Mr. Bingley said cheerfully. "I'll let you take me under your wing, then."

Darcy shook his head, pitying the affable young man. Who knew what terrible advice Wickham would give, all the while taking Mr. Bingley for every penny he could get. It would almost be worth marrying Anne simply to be able to influence George Darcy against Wickham and his copious spending.

Almost.

Mr. Bingley held up the books. "I'll get these, Darcy."

"Don't you want to know how much they'll run you?" Wickham asked before Darcy could speak. "You want to make certain he doesn't take advantage of you." He smirked at Darcy.

Mr. Bingley chuckled. "Can't see as a fine fellow with the Darcy name would swindle anyone. I'll take them regardless of the cost."

"Very well," Darcy said stiffly. No matter how many years he'd been at his bookselling business, nor how much he truly needed funds, it always dismayed him to accept payment. He'd rather gift the books to Mr. Bingley. As things stood, he gave the man a discount to make up, in some small way, for the money Wickham would separate him from.

After Mr. Bingley made his purchase the two said their goodbyes, Wickham trailing his new friend out. He paused at the door, letting it swing closed behind Mr. Bingley, and looked back to say, "I'll report to your father that you remain stubbornly opposed to bettering your circumstances, then, shall I?"

"Do what you like," Darcy replied. "You always do."

Wickham grinned. "Yes. I do, don't I?" With a parting smirk, he left.

Through the shop window, Darcy watched the two stride away. Both were fashionably dressed. Both appeared to be gentlemen. Not that Wickham ever would be, no matter how much he spent on his clothes. Darcy only hoped he didn't fleece his new friend too badly. Charles Bingley seemed like a good, if overly trusting, sort of fellow.

Shaking his head, Darcy climbed back up on the ladder and returned to dusting. At least Wickham's visit had put a bit of money in the till. Not enough to be worth Wickham's badgering, but enough to eat for a week which, added to what Darcy had, would see him into the new year. Perhaps with the influx that would come with the Christmas season, he'd be set until March, when he and his cousin Richard would take their annual pilgrimage to visit their Uncle Lewis at Rosings, to endure his list of their failings and

Anne's endless badgering for them to hunt with her.

The visit was always a strain, but a welcome break from the bookshop and a nice augmentation to Darcy's diet. He would eat more meat in one week at Rosings than during the remainder of the year, most of it hunted and brought down by Anne. As an added boon, after a week with her and Sir Lewis, Darcy's resolve to defy his father would be bolstered and he would be longing for the quiet occupation of his bookshop.

That thought in mind, he cheerfully dusted. His thoughts turned to the happier topic of the upcoming Yuletide and the influx of purchases he always saw at the end of the year. Who knew what new delights the year's end might bring?

I hope you enjoyed this sneak peek of *Mr. Darcy's Bookshop*, and I think you can guess what delights December might bring (Elizabeth. . . it's Elizabeth!)

Try *Mr. Darcy's Bookshop* today!

ABOUT THE AUTHOR

Summer Hanford writes swashbuckling Historical Romance, best-selling *Pride and Prejudice* retellings, and gripping Epic Fantasy. She lives in the Finger Lakes Region of New York with her husband and compulsory, deliberately spoiled, cat. The newest addition to their household, an energetic setter-shepherd mix, has been trying, and failing, for six years to gain acceptance from the cat, but is adored by the humans.

Since the moment she read her first novel, Summer's passion has always been writing. As a child growing up on a dairy farm, she built castles made of hay and wielded swords made of fence posts. She is also passionate about animals, travel, and organizing her closet. Nothing pleases her more than a row of tops broken down by sleeve length and ordered by color...except working on her latest novel with her cat in her lap, her dog lounging on the rug dreaming of squirrels, and a cup of tea at hand.

For more about Summer, visit
www.summerhanford.com.

Sign Up for My Mailing List Today at:
www.summerhanford.com/ pride-and-prejudice-variations

www.ingramcontent.com/pod-product-compliance
Lightning Source LLC
Chambersburg PA
CBHW020628160726
47991CB00002B/946